The Adventures of Riley the Museum Dog

Story by Devra First

Illustrations by Ryan Huddle

E
FIRST

For Julian, who read it first.
D. F.

For Aprill, Riker, and Mae.
I could never have done it without you.
R. H.

The Boston Globe, 1 Exchange Place, Suite 201
Boston, MA 02109-2132.

British Library Cataloguing-in-Publication
Information available.

Library of Congress
Cataloging-in-Publication Data available.

Printed in U.S.A.   ISBN 978-1-63076-360-2

The MFA is a great place for kids!

Full of art and discoveries, the Museum welcomes kids
and their grown-ups. Fascinating history awaits, from
mummies to model ships, and exhibitions that are friendly
to the smallest visitors and school-aged kids. We have
activities for kids of all ages right here to explore.

Visit mfa.org for more information and plan a visit today.

For information about special discounts available for bulk
purchases, sales promotions, fund-raising and educational
needs, contact Muddy Boots at 1-800-462-6420.

muddy boots
we jump in puddles

An imprint of The Rowman & Littlefield Publishing Group, Inc.
4501 Forbes Blvd., Ste. 200
Lanham, MD 20706
www.rowman.com

There was a mystery afoot at the Museum of Fine Arts in Boston.

First a hole appeared here, then a tiny bite there.

In the mummy room, somebody
nibbled on Nesmutaatneru!

Who could get to
the bottom of this?

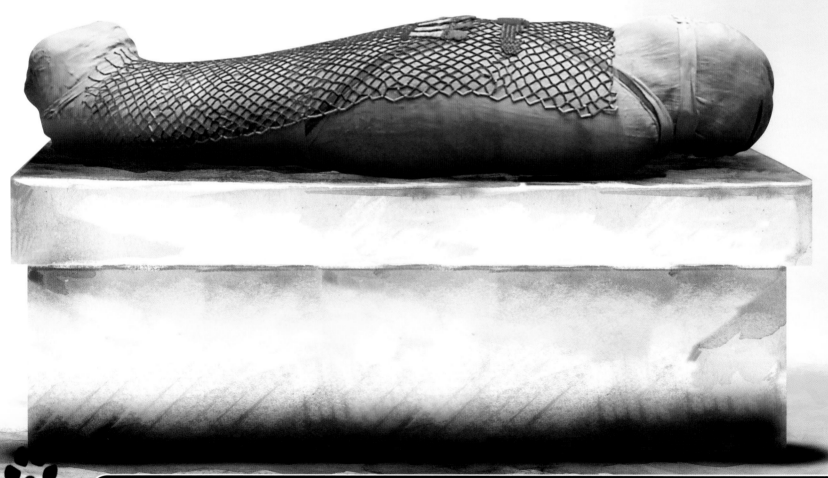

Mummy of Nesmutaatneru, Egyptian

A dog named
Riley.

Riley works at the museum. His job is to sniff out hungry pests.

What are they hungry for? Art.

When are they hungry? All of the time.

Pests think art is delicious. They appreciate a nice drawing, but they definitely think it looks better with a few bites missing.

All dogs have their strengths.
These include taking naps,
eating snacks, and chasing balls.
Riley is good at those things.

But he is best at sniffing.
Riley helps protect the art by
using his nose to find pests
before their next snack.

What do insects smell like?

How about mice?

Riley's trainers helped him learn to recognize the scents of certain pests. Now he can search a room to find them.

He sniffs back and forth, back and forth, getting closer and closer. Finally, he looks at his trainers and lies down. That's how he tells them:

"Found it!"

The Museum of Fine Arts is called the MFA for short. It is filled with ancient treasures and beautiful paintings and many other wondrous things — almost 500,000 works of art in all.

That is a lot of sniffing.

Sniff sniff sniff sniff

"… WHAT IS THAT SMELL?"

There was a lot going on in the museum, smellwise. Riley could smell pizza cooking in the cafeteria. He could smell the cookie crumbs on the shirt of a little girl who stopped in for a snack at the museum's café. He could smell the treats his trainer kept in a jar locked behind a closed door.

"Did somebody say treats?"

Stay focused, Riley, stay focused.

That smell was new.
That smell was fresh.
That smell was a pest.

This is Wiley.

She is a tiny moth, but she has a very big appetite. She lives in the MFA, which to us is a museum filled with ancient treasures and beautiful paintings and many other wondrous things.

To Wiley, it is a buffet.

A buffet with 500,000 different dishes.

She hopes one day to taste them all.

Wiley has goals.

"Excuse me, but I'm going to have to ask you to leave. You are a pest, and you have been eating the art."

"Me? Oh, how could you say that? I would never do such a thing."

Wiley waggled her antennae.

"You have a little crumb of mummy on your lip. Right there."

"I confess! I did it! The art is so delicious, I just can't help myself. I'll turn myself in, I will. Just as soon as I have lunch."

And with that, Wiley flew away, Riley sniffing close behind.

9

"Mm mm mmm.
This will be my first course.
Doesn't it look tasty?"

"Well, I guess it does kind of look like spaghetti."

"And now I am going to catch you."

"Bet you're sorry you never learned how to fly, huh?"

"But I learned how to be patient," Riley said. "What goes up must come down, and then I am going to catch you."

"What a good dog!"

Carousel figure of a greyhound, Charles I. D. Looff

"Don't. Tell him. Where I am."

"I can see you, you know. *And now I am going to catch you.*"

Dos Mujeres (Salvadora y Herminia), Frida Kahlo

"I think they'd like to have a pet dog. Stay!"

"I only stay when my trainer tells me to. It helps if treats are involved. *And now I am going to catch you.*"

Three Sisters of the Copeland Family, William Matthew Prior

HA HA HA
  HA HA HA
HA HA HA
  HA HA HA
    HA HA HA HA

"Did you see what she did to the cat?"

"This is a pretty cool three-headed mask, isn't it?"

"Three heads, but just one stomach. Very strange," Riley said. **"And now I am going to catch you."**

Little Miss Hone, Samuel F.B. Morse

Double mask, Nigerian

"That ... that's not a real door."

"Are you OK? That looked like it hurt," Riley said. "It's a *painting* of a real door. The artist, Georgia O'Keeffe, used to relax on that patio with her dogs. There's no time for relaxing now, though. I am still going to catch you."

"DANCE PARTY!"

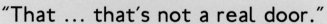

"SHAAAAARK!"

"Stay away from its teeth!
Jump away from the painting!"
Riley cried. "I will catch you!"

Watson and the Shark, John Singleton Copley

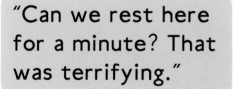
"Can we rest here for a minute? That was terrifying."

"OK, but just for a minute. *Then I am going to catch you.*"

"Lime-green icicles sound delicious, but my trainer taught me not to lick the art."

Good boy, Riley.

Lime Green Icicle Tower, Dale Chihuly

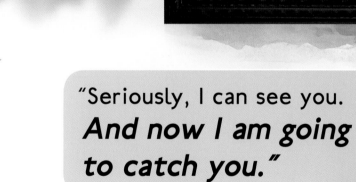

"Don't. Tell him. Where I am."

"Seriously, I can see you. *And now I am going to catch you.*"

"Torpedo" pedal car, Viktor Schreckengost

"Looks like you ran out of gas. I've got you now, pest!

I told you I was going to catch you."

"That was kind of fun," Riley said.

"It was," Wiley said.

"I have an idea," Riley said.

23

Tenshin-en, the Japanese garden

On nice days, the two would spend time together outdoors. Riley was trained to be calm in the museum, but he still needed plenty of exercise. He'd put Wiley on his back, and together they'd run and play. Wiley discovered leaves are almost as tasty as art, and she made sure not to eat the special plants that grow in the garden.

When it was rainy or cold, the two would meet inside the museum and admire the art.

Striding lion, Babylonian

The Tea, Mary Cassatt

Pictorial quilt, Harriet Powers

"Now *that's* a work of art."

Arno, Horatio Greenough

Riley had sniffed
out a pest.

But what he really
found was a friend.

Guide to Artwork

All works of art in this book are in the collection of the Museum of Fine Arts, Boston, but might not always be on view. When you visit the MFA, be sure to check in at the Sharf Visitor Center to ask whether the work of art you want to see is on view. To learn more, visit www.mfa.org.

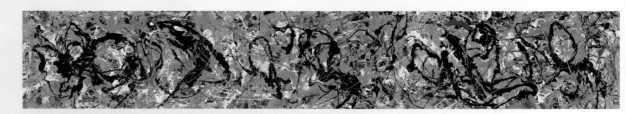

Jackson Pollock, American, 1912–1956
Number 10, 1949, 1949
Alkyd (synthetic paint) and oil on canvas mounted on panel
46.04 x 272.41 cm (18 ⅛ x 107 ¼ in.)
Tompkins Collection—Arthur Gordon Tompkins Fund and Sophie M. Friedman Fund
1971.638
© 2019 Pollock-Krasner Foundation / Artists Rights Society (ARS), New York

Page 10

Samuel Finley Breese Morse, American, 1791–1872
Little Miss Hone, 1824
Oil on canvas mounted on plywood
76.52 x 63.82 cm (30 ⅛ x 25 ⅛ in.)
Bequest of Martha C. Karolik for the M. and M. Karolik Collection of American Paintings, 1815–1865
48.455

Page 16

Kehinde Wiley, American, born in 1977
John, 1st Baron Byron, 2013
Oil on canvas
Framed: 208.6 x 178.3 cm (82 ⅛ x 70 ¼ in.)
Juliana Cheney Edwards Collection, The Heritage Fund for a Diverse Collection and funds donated by Stephen Borkowski in honor of Jason Collins
2013.633
© Kehinde Wiley Studio

Page 21

John Singleton Copley, American, 1738–1815
Watson and the Shark, 1778
Oil on canvas
183.51 x 229.55 cm (72 ¼ x 90 ⅜ in.)
Gift of Mrs. George von Lengerke Meyer
89.481

Page 18

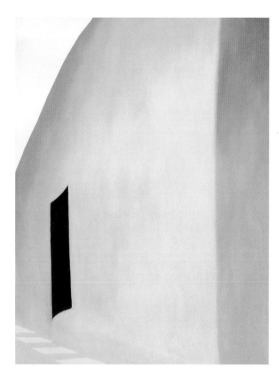

Jonathan Borofsky, American, born in 1942
I Dreamed I Could Fly, 2000
Fiberglass, acrylic paint (one figure with electric light)
157.5 x 91.4 cm (62 x 36 in.)
Museum purchase with funds donated by Hank and Lois Foster
2001.269.1
Reproduced with permission

Page 12

Frida Kahlo, Mexican, 1907–1954
Dos Mujeres (Salvadora y Herminia), 1928
Oil on canvas
69.5 x 53.3 cm (27 ⅜ x 21 in.)
Charles H. Bayley Picture and Paintings Fund, William Francis
Warden Fund, Sophie M. Friedman Fund, Ernest
Wadsworth Longfellow Fund, Tompkins
Collection—Arthur Gordon Tompkins Fund, Gift of Jessie H.
Wilkinson—Jessie H. Wilkinson Fund, and Robert M.
Rosenberg Family Fund
2015.3130
© 2019 Banco de México Diego Rivera Frida Kahlo Museums
Trust, Mexico, D.F. / Artists Rights Society (ARS), New York.

Page 14

Georgia O'Keeffe, American, 1887–1986
Patio with Black Door, 1955
Oil on canvas
101.6 x 76.2 cm (40 x 30 in.)
Gift of the William H. Lane Foundation
1990.433
© 2019 Georgia O'Keeffe Museum / Artists Rights Society
(ARS), New York

Page 17

Paul Gauguin, French, 1848–1903
Where Do We Come From? What Are We?
Where Are We Going? 1897–98
Oil on canvas
139.1 x 374.6 cm (54 ¾ x 147 ½ in.)
Tompkins Collection—Arthur Gordon Tompkins Fund
36.270

Page 19

Harriet Powers, American, 1837–1910
Pictorial quilt, 1895—98
Cotton plain weave, pieced, appliqued,
embroidered, and quilted
175 x 266.7 cm (68 ⅞ x 105 in.)
Bequest of Maxim Karolik
64.619

Page 30

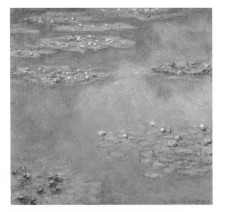

Claude Monet, French, 1840–1926
Water Lilies, 1907
Oil on canvas
96.8 x 98.4 cm (38 ⅛ x 38 ¾ in.)
Bequest of Alexander Cochrane
19.170

Page 29

Mary Stevenson Cassatt, American, 1844–1926
The Tea, about 1880
Oil on canvas
64.77 x 92.07 cm (25 ½ x 36 ¼ in.)
M. Theresa B. Hopkins Fund
42.178

Page 28

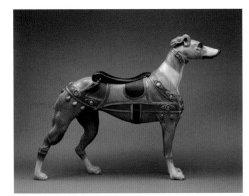

Charles I. D. Looff, 1852–1918
Carousel figure of a greyhound
Object Place: Providence, Rhode Island,
United States, about 1905–10
Painted wood; glass
137.16 x 38.1 x 185.42 cm (54 x 15 x 73 in.)
Gift of Claire M. and Robert N. Ganz
1992.267

Page 13

"Torpedo" pedal car
designed about 1937–49
Object Place: Cleveland, Ohio
Designed by: Viktor Schreckengost, American, 1906–2008
Manufactured by: Murray Ohio Company, active 1919–1988
Steel, chrome, enamel
Length: 94 cm (37 in.)
Museum purchase with funds donated by J. Parker Prindle in the
name of Carson Edwin Prindle
2010.29
Viktor Schreckengost ™ with permission from American da Vinci, LLC

Page 22

William Matthew Prior, American, 1806–1873
Three Sisters of the Copeland Family, 1854
Oil on canvas
68.26 x 92.71 cm (26 ⅞ x 36 ½ in.)
Bequest of Martha C. Karolik for the M. and M. Karolik
Collection of American Paintings, 1815—1865
48.467

Page 15

Mummy of Nesmutaatneru
Egyptian, Late Period, Dynasty 25,
760–660 B.C.
Findspot: Egypt, Thebes, Deir el-Bahari,
Temple of Hatshepsut
Human remains, linen, faience
Length: 151 cm (59 ½ in.)
Egypt Exploration Fund by subscription
95.1407a

Page 2

**Pierre-Auguste Renoir, French,
1841–1919**
Dance at Bougival, 1883
Oil on canvas
181.9 x 98.1 cm (71 ⅝ x 38 ⅝ in.)
Picture Fund
37.375

Page 17

Artist Unidentified
Double mask (enyi ima)
Eket, 19th–20th century
Object Place: Nigeria
Wood, pigment, fiber
52.5 x 28 cm (20 ⅝ x 11 in.)
Frank B. Bemis Fund
1992.510

Page 16

Dale Chihuly
Lime Green Icicle Tower, 2010
1295.7 x 213.4 cm (42 ½ x 7 ft.)
Museum of Fine Arts, Boston, installed 2011
Museum purchase made possible by a major
leadership gift from The Donald Saunders
and Liv Ullmann Family for The
People of Boston, with additional gifts from
Irving W. Rabb, Dr. Lawrence H. and Roberta
Cohn, Penny and Jeff Vinik,
Matthew A. and Susan B. Weatherbie
Foundation, John F. Cogan, Jr. and Mary L.
Cornille, Vance Wall Foundation,
Robert and Jane Burke, Mr. and Mrs. J.
Richard Fennell, Mr. and Mrs. George D.
Behrakis, Mr. and Mrs. Gerald R.
Jordan, Jr., Alan, S. and Lorraine D. Bressler,
Bettina and Craig Burr, Dale A. Roberts, funds
donated in honor of Gerald
W. R. Ward, Katharine Lane Weems Senior
Curator of Decorative Arts and Sculpture
(1992—2011), and funds donated
anonymously and by contribution from more
than one thousand individuals
2011.1634
© 2010 Chihuly Studio

Page 20

Horatio Greenough, American, 1805–1852
Arno
Object Place: Florence, Italy, 1839
Marble
64.1 x 130.8 x 57.2cm (25 ¼ x 51 ½ x 22 ½ in.)
Arthur Tracy Cabot Fund
1973.601

Page 31

Striding lion
Near Eastern, Mesopotamian, Babylonian
Neo-Babylonian Period, reign of Nebuchadnezzar I
604–561 B.C.
Findspot: Babylon, Iraq
Glazed bricks
Height: 106 cm (41 ¾ in.); width: 232 cm (91 ⅜ in.)
Maria Antoinette Evans Fund
31.898

Page 27

Hi

My name is Riley and I am a volunteer at the MFA. Volunteer critter catcher, that is. My strong sense of smell makes it easier for me to sniff out bugs and other pests that like to eat canvas and wood — even before my friends the conservators can see them — to save the art in the museum's collection from being damaged. It's hard work, but I love my trainers, Nicki and Chris, who are teaching me how to be a good dog and what to sniff for. I live with Nicki and her family — Lori, Jack, Jake, Maddie, and Kenzie. I call my job at the MFA volunteering because those kids are work! And I make sure they know how much work it is to have an active dog like me. I celebrated my first birthday recently and my vet, Dr. Brian at Boston Veterinary Clinic, says I am still growing strong! I hope you enjoy my story and follow me at #RileyTheMuseumDog to keep up to date on my adventures.

Woof!